W9-BFJ-592

DISCARDED AND
WITHDRAWN FROM
WARWICK PUBLIC
LIBRARY

On a Hot, Hot Day

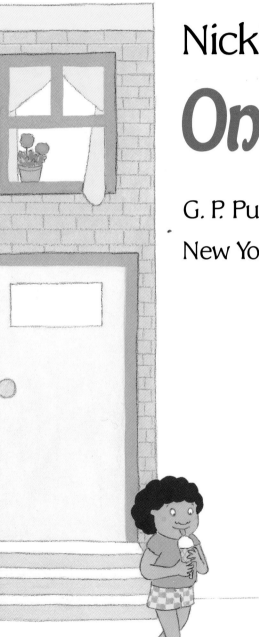

Nicki Weiss

On a Hot, Hot Day

G. P. Putnam's Sons

New York

3 2080 00241 1100

Text and illustrations copyright © 1992 by Monica J. Weiss
All rights reserved. This book, or parts thereof, may not be reproduced
in any form without permission in writing from the publisher.
G. P. Putnam's Sons, a division of The Putnam & Grosset Book Group,
200 Madison Avenue, New York, NY 10016. Published simultaneously in Canada.
Printed in Hong Kong by South China Printing Co. (1988) Ltd.
Designed by Nanette Stevenson and Colleen Flis.
The text is set in Bryn Mawr Book.

Library of Congress Cataloging-in-Publication Data
Weiss, Nicki. On a hot, hot day / Nicki Weiss.   p.   cm.
Summary: Mother and young son affectionately enjoy activities
together during each season of the year.
[1. Mothers and sons—Fiction.   2. Seasons—Fiction.]   I. Title.
PZ7.W448146on   1992   91-13234 CIP AC   [E]—dc20
ISBN 0-399-22119-0
10 9 8 7 6 5 4 3 2 1
First impression

For Zvia, Amikam, Rachel, Matan, Hadas, and Itai

On a hot, hot day
On a hot summer day

Mama says, "Think cool. Think cool."

So they spray their arms and toes and knees,
And pretend they're wading in the icy seas.

In the summer
The hot, hot summer
Mama swings her Angel.

On a rainy day
On a rainy fall day

Mama says, "Sip slow. Sip Slow."

So they blow on their cocoa in the luncheonette,
As the passersby outside get wet.

In the fall
The rainy fall
Mama twirls her Angel.

On a cold, cold day
On a cold winter day

Mama says, "Bundle up. Bundle up."

Then they shake the snow from their coats and hair,
And read all day in the big green chair.

In the winter
The cold, cold winter
Mama rocks her Angel.

On a breezy day
On a breezy spring day

Mama says, "Breathe deep. Breathe deep."

So they smell the mint and chive and dill
That Mama planted on the windowsill.

In the spring
The breezy spring
Mama hugs her Angel.

On any old day
At the end of the day

Mama says, "Good night. Sleep tight."

And she gives a hug, a twirl, a swing,
And tucks him in and starts to sing:

"Summer, fall, winter, spring—
Mama loves her Angel."

arwick Public Library
Norwood Branch
awtuxet Ave., Warwick, RI

OCT 5 1992